Reggie

Queen of the Street

Margaret Barbalet

Illustrated by
Andrew McLean

PUFFIN BOOKS

To Sonya – M.B.

PUFFIN BOOKS

Published by the Penguin Group
Penguin Group (Australia)
250 Camberwell Road,
Camberwell, Victoria 3124, Australia
(a division of Pearson Australia Group Pty Ltd)
Penguin Group (USA) Inc.
375 Hudson Street, New York, New York 10014, USA
Penguin Group (Canada)
90 Eglinton Avenue East, Suite 700, Toronto, ON M4P 2Y3, Canada
(a division of Pearson Penguin Canada Inc.)
Penguin Books Ltd
80 Strand, London, WC2R 0RL, England
Penguin Ireland
25 St Stephen's Green, Dublin 2, Ireland
(a division of Penguin Books Ltd)
Penguin Books India Pvt Ltd
11, Community Centre, Panchsheel Park, New Delhi – 110 017, India
Penguin Books (NZ)
Cnr Airborne and Rosedale Roads, Albany, Auckland, New Zealand
(a division of Pearson New Zealand Ltd)
Penguin Books (South Africa) (Pty) Ltd
24 Sturdee Avenue, Rosebank, Johannesburg 2196, South Africa

Penguin Books Ltd, Registered offices: 80 Strand, London, WC2R 0RL, England

First published by Penguin Books Australia, 20003
This edition published by Penguin Group (Australia),
a division of Pearson Australia Group Pty Ltd, 2005

10 9 8 7 6 5 4 3

Cover designed by Deborah Brash © Penguin Group (Australia)
Text designed by Susannah Low © Penguin Group (Australia)
Typeset in 17/30 pt Stone Serif
Printed and bound by Everbest Printing Co. China

National Library of Australia
Cataloguing-in-Publication data:

Barbalet, Margaret 1949– .
Reggie, queen of the street.

ISBN 0 14 350091 0

1. Dogs – Juvenile fiction.
2. Moving, Household – Juvenile fiction. I. McLean, Andrew, 1946– . II. Title.

A823.3

www.puffin.com.au

Reggie had everything in the street worked out.

There was someone to walk with.

And someone to throw a ball.

Reggie loved Doug and
Helen, but they were
not keen on walks.

They never threw a ball.

They didn't even know where the park was.
But Reggie never complained.

Helen never forgot to feed Reggie, and Doug never forgot to pat her. They never forgot to let her in. Or let her out.

'Little queen, our very own Regina,' they would whisper in a voice reserved for very loved dogs.

At night, Reggie liked to lie in her own special
spot in the study, watching them read.

But when it came to life in the dog world, Reggie always did that for herself.

Every day she walked along the street checking for messages on posts. And every day the big sheepdog ran to his gate and barked, and Reggie barked back.

Reggie was a small dog but the whole street
was hers. All the children were her friends.
She even played cricket in the park.

She was Reggie, Regina, Queen of the street.

Then one day, everything changed.

Doug and Helen packed up their books.

They were moving.

Reggie watched the children playing in the park as Doug and Helen drove away from her street. Why did they have to move?

The new house was old and the garden was bigger.

That evening, Helen set up Reggie's cane bed in the laundry.
Doug gave her more dinner. But Reggie did not care.

She woke up the next morning feeling low.

Helen called her outside and walked around the garden,
talking about what they would plant.

Reggie did not hear. That night she went to bed without
touching her dinner. But sleep would not come.

Late that night Reggie went outside.

She squeezed under the gate and walked up the hill. She could see the city below, dark and gold-lit. It looked very far away.

She set off down the hill. It took a long, long time to reach the city.

Reggie wondered if she was lost, but she could smell the way.

She just padded on and on, and on. Dogs barked at her.

Cats stared from behind fences. Cars flashed lights at her.

Around midnight, Reggie began to smell her street.

She bounced along, past all the houses, to the best one. Home!

But there was something terribly wrong. The garage and the back veranda had vanished.

Reggie walked silently past the machine and around to the back of the house. The laundry door banged in the breeze. Newspapers danced on the floor in the strange light.
Full of fear, Reggie slid inside.

This was not home. This was a dark and shaky house.
The wind slid through windows where once glass had shone.
Reggie hurried outside, her tail drooping. Somewhere she
heard an ambulance. The sheepdog down the street began
to howl with the siren. All the houses were dark.

Reggie was really tired. But she would have
to find her way back to her new home.

She set off toward the hills. All she could think
of was the house where Helen and Doug slept.
Her legs took over and trotted on and on.

After a long time, she began to think about
her dinner still sitting in her own special bowl.
Then she could think of nothing except walking.

Toward dawn, after several wrong turns, she arrived at the new street. There was the house and its garden. She limped up the path, in through the back door, and slumped in her bed, too tired to even nibble at her dinner.

When she awoke, Helen and Doug were kneeling beside
her bed in their work clothes. Doug had a fresh dish of food.
They patted her, smiling dog language.

Late in the afternoon, Reggie went into the
front garden, carrying her ball in her mouth.
Her legs hurt, but she waited.

After a while a bus came slowly up the hill.

Every time it stopped, a child jumped off.

Sometimes two or three.

A short time later, the street was alive with children.

Reggie crept under the gate and waited patiently.

A boy stopped and bent down politely to Reggie's level.

'Hello, dog,' he said. Reggie wagged her tail.

Two more children stopped. One girl put
her hand on Reggie's collar and read the tag.
'Reggie,' the girl said.

Reggie wagged her tail and trotted toward the park.
A few bigger kids were just coming out with a cricket bat.
Reggie sat on the outer field, as she always did.

By chance, the ball came
her way. Reggie leapt.
Reggie twisted. She caught it!
The children stared.
As she had learnt,
Reggie carried the ball . . .

. . . back to the bowler and dropped it at his feet.

'Cool dog,' the bowler laughed.

All the children clapped.

She was Reggie, Regina, Queen of the street once more.